Dear Boys and Girls:

This is a little part of a big book called *The Black Stallion* which I hope you will read when you get older.

Your friend,

Walter Farley

THE
BLACK STALLION

**An easy-to-read adaptation
by Walter Farley**

Illustrated by Sandy Rabinowitz

BEGINNER BOOKS
A Division of Random House, Inc.

Text copyright © 1986 by Walter Farley. Illustrations copyright © 1986 by Sandy Rabinowitz. All rights re-
served under International and Pan-American Copyright Conventions. Published in the United States by
Random House, Inc., New York, and simultaneously in Canada by Random House of Canada Limited,
Toronto.

Library of Congress Cataloging-in-Publication Data: Farley, Walter. The black stallion. SUMMARY: Young
Alec Ramsay is shipwrecked on a desert island with a horse destined to play an important part in
his life. 1. Horses—Juvenile fiction. [1. Horses—fiction.] I. Rabinowitz, Sandy, ill. II. Title.
PZ10.3.F22Bl 1986 [E] 85-19927 ISBN: 0-394-86876-5 (trade); 0-394-96876-X (lib. bdg.)
Manufactured in the United States of America 1 2 3 4 5 6 7 8 9 0

GROLIER
BOOK CLUB EDITION

Far across the sea
there lived a big black horse.
He was a wild, wild horse.
The horse had a long tail,
a long mane, and long legs.
He had no name.
He was just called the Black.

One day the Black was caught!
Men tied ropes to him
and put a cloth over his eyes.
They put him on a ship.

The Black wanted to stay free.
He rose up on his hind legs
and kicked and screamed.
The men used whips.
A boy named Alec was going home
alone on the ship.
He felt sorry for
the big black horse.

The Black was kept tied
in a stall.
Every night Alec left sugar
on the stall door.
The Black never let Alec
see him.
But every morning
the sugar was gone.

One night the Black
came out.
He ate the sugar
while Alec watched.
Alec was happy.
Maybe the Black
would trust him!

That same night there was
a bad storm.
The ship rocked and tossed.
Alec put on his life jacket
and went on deck.
People were running to
the lifeboats.

"The ship is sinking!"

someone shouted.

Alec thought of the Black.

He was locked in a stall.

The horse could not escape!

Alec ran to the stall.

The Black had broken the ropes.

He was snorting and stomping.

His eyes were full of fear.

The Black must be given
a chance to live too!
Alec opened the stall door.
The horse came rushing out.
Alec tried to move away—
but he was too late!

The Black ran to the rail
and jumped into the water.
His big body pushed Alec
into the water too.

A moment later there was
a loud explosion.
The ship was sinking.
The lifeboats were gone.
Alec saw a rope in the water
and grabbed it.
The rope was tied to
the Black's halter.

The boy felt weak.

But the horse was strong.

The Black swam all night.

He pulled Alec with him.

In the morning Alec saw land.
The Black had found
a white sandy beach.
The Black had saved his life!

They were alone on an island.
They were both very thirsty.
Alec did not know how to find
fresh water.
But the Black knew how.
Alec followed him
to a small pond.
They drank and drank.

They were both very hungry.
Alec ate a few berries.

Then he picked up pieces
of driftwood.

He built a small shed.

He was still hungry.

The Black was hungry too.

How would they find more food?

Sea moss!

It grew on the rocks.

It was everywhere.

Alec gathered some.

He washed off the salt.

He dried it in the sun.

It tasted all right.

The Black liked it too.

Alec gave the Black
sea moss every day.
The horse began to
trust the boy.
One day he let Alec
climb on his back!

Alec rode the Black
up and down the beach.
What a horse!
He was as wild as
the wind—and just as fast.

From then on Alec rode
the Black every day.
He loved that horse.
He wanted to take him home.
Home!
How would they ever
get off the island?

One night it was cold.

Alec made a fire.

He crawled into the shed.

He went to sleep.

The wind blew.
Sparks from the fire
fell on the shed.
The shed began to burn.
The Black saw the flames
and screamed.
His screams woke up Alec.

Alec escaped.
But he could not put out
the fire.
It burned all night long.

Morning came.

Alec looked out to sea
and shouted.

There was a ship!

Men were coming in a boat.

They had seen the fire.

"We are going home!"

Alec shouted to the Black.

Alec got in the boat.
The men began to row.
They were afraid
of the big horse.
"We can't take him,"
they said.
"He is wild."

Alec would not leave
the Black on the island.
The Black would die.
Alec called out,
"Swim, Black, swim!"

The Black loved the boy.

He leaped into the water.

He swam after the boat.

He swam to be with Alec.

lec shouted to the sailors,
elp him! He is in trouble!
elp him aboard."
he sailors threw a long strap
to the water.

Alec swam underwater.
He put the strap
under the Black's stomach.

The sailors pulled up
the strap.
Up came the Black!
"Good boy!" said Alec.

Alec stayed with the Black
on the ship.
He fed him good food.
Oats, hay, apples!
The Black loved apples.

The ship was sailing
to America.
Alec was going home.
He was worried.
Would he be able to
keep the Black?

Alec's parents met him
at the dock.
They were very glad
to see him.
But they were afraid
of the horse.

"He is so big and wild!"
they said.
"He saved my life,"
said Alec.
Suddenly the Black poked
Alec's mother.
She jumped!

Then Alec's mother laughed.
The Black had found
an apple in her pocket.
She patted the horse.
Now Alec knew that
everything would be all right.
The Black was his!